Jessamyn = Jessica?

"*Was* Jessamyn happy with the circus?" I asked Mom.

"Oh, yes," Mom said. "She became a famous show rider and went all over the country with the circus. Her dream came true."

I turned to Elizabeth. "See?" I said. "The story has a happy ending, after all."

Elizabeth's frown turned into a smile. "Yeah, I guess it does," she said.

"And that's the whole story," Mom said. "Now, I think it's your bedtime."

Elizabeth and I headed up to our room. "Wow," Elizabeth said. "Our great-great-grandmother was really something, huh?"

"Yeah!" I said. I pretended I was waving to a circus crowd. "She was just like me!"

Bantam Books in the SWEET VALLEY KIDS series

SWEET VALLEY KIDS

THE AMAZING JESSICA

Written by
Molly Mia Stewart

Created by
FRANCINE PASCAL

Illustrated by
Ying-Hwa Hu

BANTAM BOOKS
NEW YORK • TORONTO • LONDON • SYDNEY • AUCKLAND

RL 2, 005-008

THE AMAZING JESSICA
A Bantam Book / August 1995

*Sweet Valley High® and Sweet Valley Kids are
trademarks of Francine Pascal*

Conceived by Francine Pascal

*Produced by Daniel Weiss Associates, Inc.
33 West 17th Street
New York, NY 10011*

Cover art by Susan Tang

ISBN: 0-553-48212-2

Published simultaneously in the United States and Canada

Bantam Books are published by Bantam Books, a division of Bantam
Doubleday Dell Publishing Group, Inc. Its trademark, consisting of the
words "Bantam Books" and the portrayal of a rooster, is Registered in the
U.S. Patent and Trademark Office and in other countries. Marca
Registrada. Bantam Books, 1540 Broadway, New York, New York 10036.

PRINTED IN THE UNITED STATES OF AMERICA

OPM   0 9 8 7 6 5 4 3 2

To Judy and Alan Adler

CHAPTER 1

The Circus Comes to Town

Hi! My name's Jessica. Jessica Wakefield. People confuse me with my sister all the time. That's because Elizabeth and I are identical twins, so we look *exactly* alike. She's got long blond hair with bangs, just like I do. She's even got the same color eyes: blue-green. Sometimes we like to dress up in the same clothes, to confuse people even more. It's fun!

Elizabeth and I are both in Mrs. Otis's second-grade class at Sweet

Valley Elementary School. Elizabeth actually *likes* going to school. She studies really hard, and she reads a lot. Elizabeth is one of the best students in the whole class. Maybe *the* best.

Not me, though. I only like school because I get to see my friends there. We pass notes and talk and stuff. As far as I'm concerned, schoolwork is *bor*-ing.

When she's not busy doing homework, Elizabeth likes to play on the Sweet Valley Soccer League. She's one of the highest scorers. There's nothing she likes better than running around in the mud. She takes riding lessons, too, at the stables.

I hate to get my clothes dirty. I'd rather play games like hopscotch and jump rope. Anyone at school can tell you I'm one of the best jump ropers around!

A lot of people are surprised how different I am from Elizabeth. They expect us to be alike just because we *look* alike.

But even though we're different, Elizabeth and I are bestest friends, and always will be. It's like that with twins.

After school one day, Elizabeth and I ran through the front door at exactly the same time. "We're home!" we shouted together.

Our mom looked at us and laughed. She was sitting in the living room, reading a magazine about country homes. Mom takes classes, because she wants to become an interior decorator.

"I guess you are," she said, smiling. "What's all the excitement about?"

I answered at the same time as Elizabeth: "The circus!"

Steven (he's our big brother—yuck!)

3

came into the room with his hands over his ears. "You don't have to tell us in stereo," he said with a smirk. Steven is two years older than me and Elizabeth. He thinks that makes him smarter than us, which just proves how dumb older brothers can be.

"The circus is in town," I said. "It's at the park."

"The first show is tonight," Elizabeth added. "Can we go, Mom? Please?"

Mom smiled and looked up at the ceiling. "I don't know. . . . I always thought the circus was kind of boring."

"Boring?" I couldn't believe Mom didn't like the circus. "But there'll be clowns, and lions, and lion *tamers* . . ."

"And elephants!" Elizabeth added. "I can't wait to see the elephants." She probably read about elephants in a book or something. "Can we all go, Mom? It'll be fun, really!"

4

Even Steven was excited now. "Can we, Mom?" he asked.

We all looked at Mom. She put her chin in her hand for a minute, as if she was thinking really hard. She said, "I don't know. . . ."

"Pleeeeeease?" I asked. I thought I'd die if she said no!

"Well," Mom said. She reached into her pocket and pulled out five orange stubs of paper. "I guess since I already bought the tickets, we might as well go."

Elizabeth and I started jumping up and down. "Yay!" we shouted. "Mom! You're the greatest!"

Steven put his hands back over his ears. "Girls are so silly," he said. "It's only the circus." But I saw him smiling as he left the room.

CHAPTER 2

The Greatest Show on Earth

"Isn't this great?" Elizabeth asked. "It sure is!" I said. The circus was about to start. We were sitting in the bleachers, right up close to the center ring. Mom and Dad sat behind us.

Suddenly the lights went out. I gasped. "It's starting!" I cried.

A spotlight flashed down in the middle of the center ring. There stood the ringmaster in a bright-red coat. He wore a top hat, and he had a whip in his hand. "Ladies and gentlemen!" he announced. "Welcome to the greatest show on earth!"

The crowd cheered. The ringmaster turned and pointed to the back of the tent.

"Ladies and gentlemen!" he said. "The Incredible Gigantro!"

The tent flaps opened, and an elephant stomped right inside. It was so big, the lady riding it looked like a doll!

"Wow!" Elizabeth said. "Have you ever seen anything so huge? I bet it weighs at least a ton!"

"Two tons!" I said.

Then we saw the baby elephants behind the big one. They were adorable, with big cute eyes.

"Mom!" I said. "Can we toss them some peanuts?"

"I don't see why not," Mom answered.

Elizabeth and I each took a handful of peanuts and threw them as hard as we could into the ring. I hit one of the baby elephants in the head.

"Sorry!" I called. But the baby elephant didn't seem to mind. He came toward our section of the bleachers and put his trunk in the air, like a big question mark.

I threw another handful of peanuts, being more careful this time. They landed at the baby's feet. He picked one up with his trunk and put it in his mouth. We watched him chew it, shell and all!

"Good shot, Jessica!" Elizabeth said. Lots of people sitting around us said the same thing. I felt like part of the show! I love being the center of attention.

Next came the jugglers. They juggled all kinds of things: rubber balls, knives, even flaming torches. I held my breath right up until they took their bows.

We all had fun laughing at the clowns next. They rode around on little bicycles and kept crashing into one another. My favorite part was when they started throwing pies at each other. I laughed so hard, my stomach hurt.

Then came the absolute *best* part of the whole circus. The lights went out again, and the tent became very quiet. Then, bursting into the spotlight, came the show ponies!

They were so beautiful! They ran around the ring, graceful as ballerinas. Their coats shone in the bright light. The women riding the ponies smiled and waved. Each one wore a bright costume, and their rhinestones sparkled.

"They're amazing!" I said. I'd never seen anything so fabulous in my whole life.

Elizabeth pointed. "Look at that girl!" she said.

On the very last pony sat a girl in a pretty red costume. Her long brown hair was tied up in a braid. Her cheeks were rosy red, and she waved to the crowd.

"She looks like she's our age!" Elizabeth said. "I wish I could ride like her."

"Me, too," I said. For a second, I wished *I* was the one taking riding lessons.

All the show riders did tricks. They stood on their ponies and rode around the ring. They even did back flips. Through hoops!

But the most incredible thing was that the little girl could do everything

11

the other riders could. She was fantastic!

At the end of their act, the show riders all held hands and took a bow in the spotlight. Then the ponies took a bow, touching their noses to the ground.

I stood up and cheered like crazy. I watched the youngest show rider wave to the crowd one last time before she rode out of the tent.

"Mom!" I said. "You know what? When I grow up, I want to be a show rider!"

Mom smiled. "You mean like your great-great-grandmother Jessamyn?"

"Who?" I said.

"Watch the show," Mom said. "I'll tell you later."

"OK," I said, but I could hardly wait.

Who was Jessamyn?

CHAPTER 3
Jessamyn

"Now, Mom?" I said. "*Now* will you tell us about Jessamyn?"

The whole family was in the living room. We had just got back from the circus. I couldn't wait any longer!

"All right, all right." Mom laughed. "I'll tell you the whole story, if you promise to sit still and listen."

"I promise!" I said.

"Me, too!" Elizabeth said. I could tell she was curious.

"This sounds boring," Steven said.

"Don't be so sure," Dad told him.

"Jessamyn was *your* great-great-grandmother, too."

"That's right," Mom said. "And she was a real adventurer."

Steven made a face. But he sat down.

"About a hundred years ago," Mom began, "there were two sisters. They were identical twins. They both had blond hair and blue-green eyes."

I gasped. "Just like us!" I said.

"A lot like you indeed," Mom said. "Which is no surprise, since one of them was Jessamyn, your great-great-grandmother. And the other sister was your great-great-grandaunt Elisabeth."

"Just like me!" Elizabeth squealed.

"Right. Although she spelled her name with an *s*, not a *z*," Mom told her. "As I was saying, these two twins grew up about a hundred years ago in a place called Prairie Lakes, Minnesota. They lived a frontier life: farming, husking corn, and gathering around the hearth fire with their family at night.

"Now, Jessamyn was the wild twin. She liked to do things the boys did, like play baseball and ride horses. Sometimes she drove her parents crazy with her antics.

"Elisabeth was the quiet sister. She liked to read whenever she could, under the shade of one of the big trees on the farm. She helped her mother keep up the house, and everyone loved her for her caring ways.

"Then one year the circus came to Prairie Lakes. Jessamyn fell in love with it at first sight. She loved the snake charmers, the strongman, and the elephants. But what she loved most was the horses.

"Jessamyn's dream was to become as good as the show riders she saw in the circus. She even took riding lessons from a Native American man she knew.

"Jessamyn was bored with the quiet life in Prairie Lakes. She promised herself that one day she would join the circus and travel all over the world, having exciting adventures.

"One morning, when the twins were both sixteen years old, Elisabeth found a note in the kitchen. It was from Jessamyn. During the night, Jessamyn had snuck away from the farm and run off with the circus. She was very sorry to leave her family, but she couldn't pass up her one chance at happiness.

"Elisabeth was very sad, of course. But her mom and dad told her that Jessamyn would be happy, living the life she'd always dreamed of living."

"Poor Elisabeth," Elizabeth said

sadly. "I don't know what I'd do if I found a note like that."

"*Was* Jessamyn happy with the circus?" I asked Mom.

"Oh, yes," Mom told us. "She became a very good show rider and went all over the country, doing her routines. Her dream came true."

I turned to Elizabeth. "See?" I said. "The story has a happy ending, after all."

Elizabeth's frown turned into a smile. "Yeah, I guess it does," she said.

"And that's the whole story," Mom said. "Now, I think it's your bedtime."

Elizabeth and I headed up to our room. "Wow," Elizabeth said. "Our great-great-grandmother was really something, huh?"

"Yeah!" I said. I pretended I was waving to a circus crowd. "She was just like me!"

I got into my pajamas and jumped onto my bed. I tried to picture Great-great-grandma Jessamyn in my mind. She looked the way I imagine I'll look when I'm sixteen. She was tall and beautiful, and she rode her horse like a princess.

I imagined Jessamyn riding into an old frontier town on her most gorgeous horse. All the townsfolk stood on the side of the road and waved their hats and bandannas. Every boy in town took one look at her and fell madly in love.

Of course, Jessamyn didn't give them a second glance. Just like me, I was sure Great-great-grandma Jessamyn *never* liked boys.

Elizabeth got into bed, too. Then Mom came to tuck us in.

"Thank you for taking us to the circus, Mom," I said. "It was the *best*."

"Yeah, Mom," Elizabeth said. "I had a good time."

"You're welcome, girls," Mom said. She kissed us good night and turned off the light. But she left the door open a crack.

I closed my eyes. I saw myself as Great-great-grandma Jessamyn. I was standing in the spotlight taking my bows. Lots of little girls like me were cheering and clapping like crazy.

I had an idea.

"Elizabeth?" I said.

"Yes, Jess?" she answered.

"From now on," I said, "you can call me Jessamyn, OK?"

I waited, but Elizabeth didn't say okay.

I rolled over and dreamed about the circus all night long.

CHAPTER 4
Call Me Jessamyn

At breakfast the next morning, I told Mom and Dad to call me Jessamyn. They just looked at each other and laughed.

"What's so funny?" I said. "I can change my name if I want, can't I?"

Steven laughed so hard, milk came out his nose. I was grossed out. Elizabeth didn't laugh. She just looked up at the ceiling and poked at her pancakes with a fork.

"Of course you can, honey," Mom said. "Whenever you like."

"Just keep us informed," Dad said with a wink.

I looked around the table. Everyone was trying hard not to smile. They weren't doing a very good job of it, either.

"I'm changing my name, too," Steven said. "I want everybody to call me Sinbad."

"Shut up," I said.

On the bus to school, I decided how to tell the kids at school about my new name. I wanted to be dramatic about it, so they wouldn't forget.

Mrs. Otis wasn't in the classroom yet. I stood up on my desk and waved my arms as I'd seen the ringmaster do. As loud as I could, I said: "May I have your attention, please!"

The whole class stopped talking and looked up at me. I loved it. I felt

as if there were a spotlight on me!

"I have an announcement!" I said. "From now on, my name is not Jessica Wakefield. My name is . . . Jessamyn!"

I saw Elizabeth frown. Everyone else just sort of stared at me. Then Mrs. Otis walked into the room. She blinked.

"Well," Mrs. Otis said with a chuckle. "Are you entertaining the class, Jessica?"

"No," I said. I felt a little silly. "And my name's not Jessica, anymore, Mrs. Otis. It's Jessamyn."

Mrs. Otis nodded thoughtfully. "I won't ask why," she said, "but if that's what you'd like to be called, that's fine with me . . . *Jessamyn*. But no matter what your name is, you're still not allowed to stand on your desk. All right?"

A few kids giggled. I hardly even noticed. Mrs. Otis was on my side! Now
everybody would call me by my new
name.

At recess I was standing by the
swings with Lila Fowler, Amy Sutton,
and Elizabeth. Amy is Elizabeth's best
friend—after me, of course. Elizabeth
was on one of the swings, but she
wasn't swinging. She just sat there.

"Jessamyn?" said Lila. She wrinkled
her nose. "Why should we call you
Jessamyn all of a sudden?"

"Because," I explained, "that was
my great-great-grandmother's name.
I'm sort of named after her."

"Jessamyn's a dumb name," Lila
said.

"It is not!" I cried. Lila is my best
friend after Elizabeth, but she can be
a real snob sometimes. "It's not half
as dumb as 'Lila'!"

Lila turned up her nose. "You're just jealous because your name's not as pretty as mine. *Either* of your names."

"I think Jessamyn's a pretty name," Amy said. She sat on the swing next to Elizabeth and pushed off. "What was your great-great-grandmother like?"

"She was awesome," I told her. "She rode horses and ran away with the circus and had all kinds of adventures."

All of a sudden Elizabeth spoke up. "And she had a twin sister, too," she said. "Her name was Elisabeth, like me. Except she spelled it with an *s*. Isn't that cool?"

"Yeah!" Amy said. "I guess twins must run in your family, huh?"

I bit my lip. I didn't want to talk about this. I wanted to talk about me.

"When I get old enough," I said, "I'm gonna be a show rider, just like Great-great-grandma Jessamyn. I'll be famous!"

"Wow!" Amy said. "Why not? It's in your blood!"

"Hey, that's right!" I said.

Lila made a face. "Who wants to join the circus? Besides, horses are smelly."

"Are not!" I said, even though I'd always thought horses were smelly before. "Besides, who cares? I'm going to wear a beautiful costume, and everybody will throw flowers."

"But, Jessica," Elizabeth said, "you don't even know how to ride a horse."

I stared at Elizabeth as hard as I could. *"Jessamyn,"* I hissed.

Elizabeth shrugged. "Whatever," she mumbled.

"Besides, it can't be that hard to

ride a horse," I said. "There's a girl our age in the circus, and she rides as good as a grown-up."

"*I* know!" Amy said. "You could take lessons with me and Elizabeth! Wouldn't that be fun?"

"I don't think I need lessons," I said. "Like you said, it's in my blood."

"Maybe you're right," Amy said. "Hey, Elizabeth, maybe someday you can *both* join the circus!"

"Maybe," Elizabeth muttered. I could tell she meant "No way."

"Was the other Elizabeth a show rider, too?" Amy asked.

"Uh-uh," I said. "She just sat around the house and did chores and read books and stuff. She was *boring*. Jessamyn was the *cool* sister."

Suddenly Elizabeth jumped off the swing and walked away in a huff.

"What's her problem?" Lila asked.

"Who knows?" I said. "She's been crabby all day."

Amy looked at me. "Maybe you said something to hurt her feelings, Jessica."

I nearly screamed: *"Jessamyn!"*

CHAPTER 5
Only Dreaming

"Yeeha! Giddyap!"

It was after school. I was riding my invisible pony around the family room. Elizabeth was sitting on the couch, watching TV.

"You'd better be careful," she said. "We're not supposed to run in the living room."

"I'm not running. I'm trotting," I told her. "What's on TV?"

"Soccer game," she said. She looked really interested.

"*Bor*-ing," I said. I pretended to do

show-rider tricks. I yelled "Yeeha!" as loud as I could.

"What was that?" Mom called from the kitchen.

"Nothing, Mom!" I called back. "It's just the TV."

All of a sudden, Elizabeth said, "How are you ever going to become a show rider if you don't take riding lessons?"

"I told you," I said. "I don't need lessons. I'll be a natural, just like Great-great-grandma Jessamyn."

"But even Jessamyn took lessons," Elizabeth pointed out. "From a real Native American, too."

She was right. I had forgotten about that. "It doesn't matter," I said after a minute. "Lessons are *bor*-ing."

"I think riding lessons are fun," Elizabeth said.

"Well," I told her, "*I'm* not *you*."

Elizabeth folded her arms and looked away. She stared at the soccer game. I wondered what was the matter with her. She wouldn't even call me Jessamyn!

I decided to do some acrobatic stuff, to show Elizabeth I was born to be in the circus. "I bet you can't do this," I said.

I went to the far side of the room and did a cartwheel behind the couch. I slipped a little on the carpet, and one of my feet knocked a lamp off a table. I landed on my bottom, and the lamp broke on the floor.

Elizabeth gasped. "Are you all right, Jess?"

"Of course I'm all right!" I snapped. "The carpet's too slippery, that's all."

All of a sudden, Mom was standing over me. "What's going on in here?" she asked.

Before I could say anything, Elizabeth answered her.

"Jessica tried to do a cartwheel and broke the lamp," she said.

Mom looked at the broken lamp and shook her head. "Jessica, you know there's no roughhousing in the house, don't you?"

"Yes, Mom," I said. "But—"

"No buts," Mom said. "Go to your room, Jessica."

There was no way out of it, so I stomped up the stairs. I was really mad at Elizabeth. Why did she have to get me into trouble like that? She didn't even give me a chance to explain.

I flopped down onto my bed and closed my eyes. Maybe Elizabeth was just jealous that I was going to be a famous circus star. *Yeah,* I thought, *that must be it.*

33

I started to daydream. I imagined that I had joined the circus. I wore my sparkly costume everywhere I went. There was never any homework to do, and I did cartwheels anyplace I wanted to.

All my neat circus friends called me Jessamyn. They treated me with the respect that a great show rider deserves. We all laughed and did tricks all day long. When we got hungry, we ate lots and lots of cotton candy.

I saw myself out in the center ring, riding my pony. All my fans sat in the bleachers and cheered me on: "Jessamyn! Jessamyn! Jessamyn . . . !"

"Jessica?"

I jumped up. I must have really fallen asleep. I was back in my boring old bedroom, and Mom was kneeling next to my bed.

"Yes?" I yawned.

"You can come downstairs now," Mom said. "I want you to set the table tonight."

"But it's not my turn!" I said. "It's Steven's turn!"

"Consider this your punishment for breaking the lamp," Mom said. She smiled a little. "Don't worry, I can fix it. After you set the table, we can forget the whole thing. All right?"

I bit my lip. At least I was going to get off easy. "OK," I said.

So much for my dream, I thought. *Now even* Mom *won't call me Jessamyn.*

I went downstairs. Elizabeth was still watching the soccer game.

"Hey, Liz!" I said. I tried to sound friendly. "Want to help me set the table?"

Elizabeth shook her head without

looking at me. "Mom said not to help you," she said.

I was really mad now. She wasn't sorry at all about getting me into trouble! But the only thing I could do was go and set the table, or else I'd be in *more* trouble.

I made sure Elizabeth got the crooked fork. Then I felt better.

CHAPTER 6

Sister Spat

The next afternoon, I was in our room reading when Elizabeth came in. "What are you doing?" she asked.

"Reading!" I said.

Elizabeth tilted her head to one side. "But you don't even *like* books," she said.

"I like this one!" I told her. "It's about the circus!"

"Oh," Elizabeth said.

I was disappointed. I'd figured that if I read a circus book—without anyone even telling me to!—Elizabeth would know I was serious about being a show rider. But it looked as if she wasn't even interested. *Nobody* took me seriously, not even my own sister.

Elizabeth grabbed a schoolbook and went to her desk.

"Do you have to do homework *all* the time?" I asked.

"Why not?" she said. She didn't look up at me. "I'm just the boring sister."

What's wrong with her? I wondered. *I never said she was boring.*

"Come on," I said. I jumped off the bed. "Let's go ride bikes."

Elizabeth looked up really fast. She smiled. "You want to?"

"Sure!" I said. "Let's go ask Mom!"

"OK!" she said.

I felt a lot better now that Elizabeth was in a good mood again. It makes me sad whenever she's in a bad mood. It must be one of those twin-sister things.

We rode to the park. When we got there, Elizabeth looked around and sighed. "I forgot the circus was still here," she said.

There didn't seem to be any people around. Then I saw a man in blue overalls come out of the big tent. He was leading a pony by the reins. The man reached into his pocket and pulled out an apple. The pony took the whole apple into his mouth and chewed it.

"Wow!" I cried. "Did you see that?"

"Yeah," Elizabeth said. She sounded bored. "They let me give apples to the horses all the time at the stables."

"When I'm a famous show rider, like Great-great-grandma Jessamyn,"

I said, "I'll have somebody take care of my horses and ponies for me. Maybe I'll even hire you!"

"Let's go home," Elizabeth said.

I tried to tell her I wasn't done looking at the circus yet, but she was already riding away. So I had to follow her. She rode really slowly, staring at the ground.

"You know," I told her, "that book about the circus is really good."

"I don't care about the circus," she said.

"What?" I said. "How can you not care about the circus?"

Elizabeth shrugged. "I just don't."

"But it's in our blood!" I said.

"Maybe it's in *your* blood," she said. "But it's not in mine."

That sounded dumb to me. I mean, if we're sisters, it *had* to be in her blood, too, right?

We rode without talking for a while. Then I got an idea.

"Check this out," I said.

First I pedaled fast for a second, to work up some speed. Then I very carefully lifted one foot up and tried to stand on my bicycle seat.

"Jessica!" Elizabeth yelled.

"Watch me!" I said.

For a second I really thought I could do it. Then I sort of lost my balance and started to tip over. I would have landed in the middle of the street, but Elizabeth caught me. My bike clanked up against hers.

"Ooooof!" she said.

"Did you see that?" I said. "I almost did it!"

"Are you crazy?" she snapped. She pushed me away. "You could have killed yourself! And you *almost* killed *me*!"

That did it. I lost my temper.

"Who asked you to catch me, anyway?" I said. "I wouldn't have got hurt! I bet I would have landed right on my feet, just like Great-great-grandma Jessamyn!"

"Jessamyn, Jessamyn, Jessamyn!" Elizabeth yelled. "That's all you talk about! I bet you'd rather have *Jessamyn* for a sister!"

"Maybe I would!" I yelled back.

I thought I saw a tear in Elizabeth's eye. She turned away. "Well, you can't!" she said.

Elizabeth got back onto her bike and pedaled home as fast as she could. I tried to catch up, but she had too much of a head start. When she ran into the house, I was right behind her.

Mom and Dad came into the room, looking concerned. "Whoa!" Dad said. "What's the matter?"

"Jessica almost crashed her bike!" Elizabeth said. "She was trying to do tricks on it!"

"I did *not* almost crash!" I yelled.

"You would have crashed if I hadn't caught you!" Elizabeth said.

"Calm down, girls!" Mom ordered us. Her face was very stern. "Jessica, were you doing tricks on your bicycle?"

I looked down at my sneakers. "Well, sort of. I was just trying to be like Great-great-grandma Jessamyn."

"Jessica," Dad said, "if you want to be a show rider like Jessamyn, that's not the way to go about it. You should take lessons, like your sister."

"You and Elizabeth could even take lessons together," Mom suggested.

I thought about it. Maybe Dad was right—maybe I *should* take lessons. Then I saw Elizabeth grinning at me, as if she'd been right all along. What a snitch!

"No way," I said. "I'd rather die."

Mom and Dad seemed disappointed. "All right, then," Dad said. "In the meantime, you're not allowed to ride your bicycle for the next week. Understood?"

It was so unfair! But I knew there was no way to win. All I could say was yes.

"You girls go wash up for dinner now," Mom said. "It'll be ready in a minute."

I waited until Elizabeth was out of the bathroom before I went in to wash my hands. While we ate dinner that night, she kept blabbing to Mom and Dad about school and other boring stuff. I *really* hated her now.

45

CHAPTER 7

Jessamyn Runs Away (Again)

I didn't say a word to Elizabeth that night, or even the next day. I was hoping she'd miss me and feel sorry for all the trouble she'd got me into.

It didn't work. At recess she just went off and talked with Amy about the stables.

Amy said, "Riding horses is my favorite thing in the whole world!"

"Mine, too," Elizabeth said. "Everybody should try it."

She looked over at me for just a

second. I pretended to check my nails. *You just wait,* I thought.

We still weren't talking when school was over. Amy's mom came and took Amy and Elizabeth to their riding lesson. I rode the bus by myself, planning. I knew what I was going to do.

When I got home, I went right up to our room. A few minutes later, there was a knock on the door. Then Mom poked her head into the room. I pretended I was reading really hard. Mom smiled and closed the door very softly.

I waited until I heard Mom get to the bottom of the stairs. Then I threw the book down and went to the closet. I found my most ragged pair of jeans and a blue denim T-shirt. If I was going to run away—just like Jessamyn—I would have to look as much like a tomboy as I could.

I sneaked down the stairs and peeked into the living room. Mom was sitting on the couch with her back to me. She was reading a magazine. I tiptoed across the room, crossing my fingers the whole time. I took a deep breath when I got to the kitchen. Made it!

I got to the back door and put my hand on the knob. Suddenly I thought: *Maybe I should leave a note.*

After all, Great-great-grandma Jessamyn had left *her* sister a note.

I thought about it. What if I left a good-bye letter and Elizabeth found it? She'd feel sorry for being so mean then!

Or maybe she wouldn't care. Maybe she'd be happy I was gone. Then she could be the *only* sister. Mom and Dad would love her twice as much!

That idea made me angry. No matter

what I did, Elizabeth would get the better deal. But then I thought, *I'll be mil-
lions of times happier than Elizabeth
when I'm in the circus. Everyone will be
nice to me there. Especially when they
see what a great rider I am!*

So I slipped out the back door as
quietly as I could.

I decided to walk to the park—after
all, Dad said not to ride my bike. I
was so excited, my teeth were chatter-
ing. OK, maybe I was scared. A little.
I didn't know what was going to
happen. But if Great-great-grandma
Jessamyn had done it, so could I. It
was in my blood!

I stopped for a second and looked
back at my house. It looked so safe.
For a second I felt like running back
before Mom even noticed I was gone.
But nobody at home understood me
anyway! And if I gave up now, I'd

feel like I was letting Jessamyn down.

So I kept going. Pretty soon I was at the park.

Just like the day before, there weren't any people around. The coast was clear, so I made a mad dash for the big tent. Before I knew it, I was inside.

There I was, right behind the same bleachers I'd sat on just the other night. The tent was dark—I had to wait for my eyes to adjust.

Suddenly the lights came on. The center ring was all lit up. I hid under the bleachers. Were they looking for me already?

But nobody grabbed me. A few seconds later, I saw someone lead a pony into the center ring. It was the young girl we'd seen riding the other night! What luck!

I ran out from behind the bleachers and went right up to her.

"Hi!" I said. "My name is Jessic— Jessamyn! And I want to be a show rider, just like you!"

CHAPTER 8

Daria

The girl stepped back in surprise. I must have spooked the pony, too, because he took off to the other side of the ring. "Oh! Um, hi," the girl said. "My name is Daria Brahms."

"Hi, Daria," I said. "I saw you do your tricks the other night. You were awesome!"

"Thanks!" Daria smiled. She relaxed. "Did you say you wanted to be a show rider?"

"Yeah!" I said. "More than anything!"

"How come?"

I told Daria all about Great-great-grandma Jessamyn. I even told her the part about Jessamyn running away from home. "I want to be just like her!" I said.

Daria looked shocked. "You mean you ran away from home?"

Oops! I didn't want to talk about that. "Can you teach me some tricks?" I asked. "I bet you're a great teacher."

"OK," Daria said. "It'll be fun. I never get to hang out with kids my own age."

She went to fetch the pony. "Watch your step, Jessamyn," she called over her shoulder.

I loved it when Daria called me Jessamyn. I was so busy thinking about my new name that I didn't listen to her. Then I stepped in something that really

53

stank. "Gross!" I said, holding my nose. I wiped my sneaker in the dirt.

Daria led the pony over to me. She was laughing. "The ponies love to leave little surprises lying around," she said. "Don't you, Tony?"

Tony the pony snorted. Now that I was right next to him, I noticed how much *he* smelled, too. I hated to admit it, but Lila was right.

"You've ridden before, right?" Daria asked.

"Well . . . of course," I said. Which was true, sort of. I mean, I'd ridden a *bike* before. Riding a horse couldn't be *that* different, could it?

"OK. Climb on," Daria said.

I stood next to the pony. He was really big. I didn't think I'd be able to get onto his back without a stepladder. But I couldn't let Daria know I didn't have any idea what

I was doing. Me, the great-great-granddaughter of Jessamyn!

So I grabbed Tony's mane and tried to pull myself up. Tony snorted and stamped his hooves on the ground. I guess he didn't like having his hair pulled.

Daria was giggling. "Here, let me help," she said.

She came up behind me and pushed. Before I knew it, I was up on Tony's back. "Whoa!" I said. It was hard not to tip over.

"Very good," Daria said. "Now ride him around the ring."

I didn't know how to do that. "Uh, why don't you *lead* him around the ring?" I said. "Just until I get used to Tony, I mean."

"Sure," Daria said.

We went around in circles, very slowly. I could feel Tony's strong

muscles underneath me. It made me nervous. What if he decided to throw me off?

And besides, I could feel every bump in his spine. Riding a pony was really uncomfortable!

I bet Jessamyn never had a sore bottom, I thought. *I bet she could do all kinds of tricks the very first time she rode a horse.*

"OK," Daria said. "Are you ready to try some tricks now?"

"I guess so," I replied.

"We'll start easy," she said. "Just try standing up."

Stand up! I thought. *I can barely sit still!*

But I tried it anyway. It was even harder on a pony than it was on a bike. After fumbling around for a few seconds, I was sort of kneeling on Tony's back.

"Daria?" I said. "Could we just slow down a little bit?"

"Sure," Daria said. She made Tony walk about half as fast as before.

But I still didn't feel safe. "Slower," I said.

I said "slower" two or three more times. Pretty soon, Tony was standing still. My head was spinning, and my stomach felt queasy.

"Are you OK?" Daria asked.

"Sort of," I said. My voice was shaky. "Can you just help me down for a second?"

Daria gave me a hand. The ground seemed to be moving under my feet. "Ohhhhh," I groaned. I felt really sick now.

"It's OK," Daria said. She put her arm around my shoulders and led me to the bleachers. "You know, Jessamyn," she said gently, "maybe you're just not cut out to be a show rider."

"I have to be!" I insisted. "It's in my blood! I *have* to join the circus! I'll do anything!"

A sad look came into Daria's eyes.

"That's funny," she said. "I'd do anything to *leave* the circus."

CHAPTER 9

Second Thoughts

I stared at Daria. *I must be hearing things,* I thought.

"You're kidding, right?" I said. "Why would anyone *ever* want to leave the circus?"

"You don't know what life in the circus is like, Jessamyn," Daria said. "We're on the road all the time. I mean, I like to travel, but I miss having a normal life."

"A normal life?" I said. "What do you mean?"

"You know. Like other kids," Daria

said. "I wish I could go to school and make friends. I have lots of friends in the circus, but they're all grown-ups. I never get to play with kids my own age."

"You know," I told her, "a normal life isn't much fun. I get bored a lot."

"Really?" Daria looked as if she was daydreaming. "I think *circus* life is boring. All we do is put on the show, pack up the trucks, and drive for a couple of days. And then we do it all over again.

"And it's *so hard* to be a show rider, I have to practice *all the time.* I never get to have any fun."

It sounded like Daria was really sad. "I want to ask my parents if I can quit the circus for a while," she said. "But I'm afraid they'll be disappointed. They work for the circus, too, and I know they're really proud of me."

"Wow!" I said. "Your mom and dad are in the circus? I bet your mom's that beautiful lady on the trapeze, right? And your dad, he must be the strongman or something, right?"

Daria burst out laughing. "Nope," she said. "Actually, my mom runs the peanut stand, and my dad helps take care of the ponies."

"Oh," I said. That didn't sound like fun. "I guess being in the circus isn't always that exciting, huh?"

Daria shook her head. "Doing the shows is fun. But besides that, it's really not glamorous at all."

We didn't say anything for a while. I was thinking of how unhappy I'd feel if I never got to hang around with my friends.

Tony the pony came over and snorted at us. Daria gave him a sugar cube. I tried to imagine working with a pony. All day. *Every* day. I'd be exhausted! Plus, I'd get *really* dirty. And if there's one thing I hate, it's getting dirt on my clothes. And . . . *stuff* on my sneakers.

"You know, Daria," I said, "it's kind of funny. You want to be me, and I want to be you. And we're both miserable."

"Yeah," Daria said. She was running her fingers through Tony's mane. "Too bad we can't change places, huh?" She looked at what I was wearing. We were dressed almost alike. "We *look* like twins, anyway," she joked.

All of a sudden I felt very, very sad. "I already *have* a twin," I told her.

Daria's eyes got as big as saucers. "Really?" she squealed. "A twin sister?"

"Uh-huh," I said.

"Wow," Daria said. She looked all dreamy again. "That must be so cool. I bet you guys are best friends, right?"

"Yeah." *Until lately,* I thought.

"I don't have any brothers or sisters," Daria sighed. "I wish I did."

I smiled. Now that I thought about it, I was a really lucky girl. I had a nice home. My folks took good care of me. I had lots of friends. And I even had a twin sister. Not many people in the world have a twin sister!

I wondered if Elizabeth had got home yet. If she had, she already knew I was gone, just like Jessamyn. Then she'd have to tell Mom . . . just like Great-great-grandaunt Elisabeth.

She'll feel awful! I thought. How could Great-great-grandma Jessamyn hurt her sister like that? Was I really *that* mad at Elizabeth?

64

Maybe I shouldn't have run away, after all. . . .

Suddenly I heard a voice outside the tent. "Jess!" the voice yelled. "Are you in there, Jess?"

CHAPTER 10
Reunion

I was terrified! If Dad caught me running away from home, he'd ground me for the rest of my life. At *least*!

The voice outside yelled: "Jessamyn! Are you in there?"

Wait a minute. Who would call me Jessamyn, besides Daria?

The tent flap opened behind me.

"Jessamyn!" Elizabeth said. "There you are!"

"Lizzie! What are you doing here?"

Elizabeth ran right over to me. She

looked really upset. "Jessamyn, don't run away! I'm sorry about everything! I won't even tell Mom and Dad you ran away, just come back, please!"

I was happy to see my sister. I couldn't believe I'd almost decided never to see her again. What was I thinking? Then I realized what she had just said. She hadn't told on me!

"You mean Mom and Dad aren't with you?" I asked.

"No," Elizabeth said. She took a deep breath. "My riding instructor twisted his ankle, so there was no lesson today. I got home really early. I went upstairs to say I was sorry for getting you in trouble, but you weren't there. When I saw you were gone, I knew you'd run away to join the circus."

Daria looked confused. "How did you know that?" she asked.

"Twins know things about each other," I said with a smile.

"Right!" Elizabeth said. "And the circus book on the bed was a good clue, too."

I realized that Daria and Elizabeth didn't know each other. I introduced them.

"Hi, Daria," Elizabeth said. "We saw you the other night. You're really good."

"Thanks," Daria said. "You look tired. Did you run all the way here?"

"Yup," Elizabeth said. "I snuck out of the house," she told me. "I thought maybe if I could find you quick, we could both get home before Mom knew we were gone."

I was amazed. "But you could get in trouble!" I said.

Elizabeth shrugged. "That's OK. I owe you a favor. I'm sorry I was so mean. I was just mad because you didn't want to take riding lessons with me."

Daria laughed. "She could sure *use* some riding lessons," she said.

Elizabeth smiled. I could tell she liked Daria. "Besides," she went on, "I don't want to be the boring sister. So I decided to do something exciting for a change."

"I'm sorry, too," I told Elizabeth. "I wanted to be like Jessamyn. But I didn't want you to think you were like Elizabeth."

"So you mean you'll come home?" Elizabeth asked.

"Sure thing," I said. I made a face. "Ponies are smelly anyway."

"Yay!" Elizabeth laughed, and gave me a big hug. Then we both felt a gust of hot breath on our faces. It was Tony the pony, nudging us with his nose.

"Tony, cut it out!" I said. "You'll smudge my shirt!"

"What a cute pony!" Elizabeth turned to Daria. "Could you do a couple of tricks for us?" she asked. "I ride horses. I'd love to see how someone really good does it."

"Sure!" Daria said. "I'll give you guys a special private show!"

"Great!" we said.

Elizabeth and I sat in the bleachers. "Hey," I said, "you called me Jessamyn!"

Elizabeth nodded. "I'll call you anything, as long as you don't run away."

I've got the best sister in the world, I thought.

Daria was already riding Tony around the ring at top speed. Her hair fluttered and waved in the breeze.

"Yay! Go, Daria!" Elizabeth yelled.

Daria stood on Tony's back. She

waved to us and smiled, as if we were a whole crowd. We clapped and cheered like crazy.

"Hey, guys, watch this!" Daria called to us. "This is my best trick!"

Daria stood still on Tony's back and closed her eyes for a second. Then she jumped way up, did a back flip, and landed right on Tony's back again.

Elizabeth and I said *"Wow!"* at the same time. We clapped till our hands were sore. Daria's face was lit up like Christmas morning.

"That was awesome!" I said. "I really wish I could be in the circus. Just once, I mean. For Great-great-grandma Jessamyn."

Elizabeth wrinkled her forehead. That's what she does when she's thinking hard.

"I have an idea," she said.

"What is it?"

"Come on," she said. "Let's talk to Daria about it."

Daria jumped off Tony the pony and did a little curtsy. "Tell me about what?" she asked.

Elizabeth explained the plan she'd thought up. We both thought it was brilliant. It was even sneaky!

When the plan was all settled, Elizabeth said: "We'd better run home, Jessica. We don't want to get caught."

"OK," I said. " 'Bye, Daria."

" 'Bye," Daria said. "Hey, wait a minute. *Jessica?* I thought your name was *Jessamyn.*"

Elizabeth and I winked at each other. "Nope," I told Daria. "It's like my sister said."

CHAPTER 11

Sneaky Sisters

Mom was still reading when we got back. What luck! Elizabeth and I tiptoed behind her as quietly as we could.

Then, without looking up, Mom called: "Jessica! Elizabeth!"

We traded glances and then raced upstairs. I hoped that Mom hadn't seen us. When we got to our bedroom, Elizabeth and I jumped onto our beds and each grabbed a book as fast as we could. We could hear Mom coming up the stairs.

When she opened the door, Mom saw us "reading," just like we were supposed to be.

"Hello, girls," she said. "Didn't you hear me call you?"

"Nope!" Elizabeth said. "I guess we were too wrapped up in what we were reading."

"Right!" I agreed. "That's what we've been doing all this time. Just reading."

"Oh. I see," Mom said. She looked at us kind of funny. "Well, I wanted to ask if you two would like to help me fix supper tonight."

"Sure!" we said.

Elizabeth caught my eye and whispered: "Ask her!"

"Oh, yeah!" I said. "Mom, can I go over to Lila's tomorrow after school?"

"I think that sounds nice," Mom said.

Elizabeth and I winked at each other. If only Mom knew!

"Well, let's head for the kitchen," Mom said.

The minute Mom left the room, Elizabeth cracked up. "Your book's upside down," she said.

We hadn't laughed so hard since the circus.

The next day, I got home just in time for supper. Elizabeth got back from her riding lesson at the same time. We washed our hands together, side by side at the bathroom sink.

"How did it go?" she whispered.

"Perfect," I whispered back. "Everything's going according to plan."

"Cool," Elizabeth said. I could tell she was just as excited as I was.

At the dinner table, Steven kept sniffing the air.

"Something smells funny," he said.

Elizabeth brushed some lint off her shirt. "Oh, it must be me," she said. "The stable smell gets into my clothes sometimes. Sorry."

"Hey, Mom," I said, as casually as I could. "Can we *please* go to the circus again?"

Steven dropped his fork and rolled his eyes. *"Again?"* he whined.

"If we go to the circus," I told Steven, "I'll do your chores for a whole week."

He turned to Mom and Dad. "Can we *please* go again?" he asked.

All three of us gave Mom and Dad our best puppy-dog looks. They threw up their hands.

"We surrender," Mom said. "Tomorrow night, we'll go again."

I gave Elizabeth a high five over the table. The plan was going great!

"Pass the beans, please," Steven said.

I handed Steven the bowl of string beans. His nose twitched. "Hey," he said. "You smell funny, too."

Uh-oh.

But Elizabeth saved the day again. She leaned over and pretended to sniff Steven's clothes. "Speak for yourself," she told Steven.

Mom and Dad laughed. I was so proud of my sister. She can be a great sneak when she wants to.

CHAPTER 12

The Grand Finale

"I think the circus is even more fun the second time around," I said to my friends. We were all back in the bleachers, watching the clowns.

"Me, too!" Amy said. "It was nice of your parents to bring us along."

"I think it's *boring* the second time," Lila said. She crinkled up her nose. "Besides, I can smell all the animals. I don't know why I let you talk me into this, Jessica."

"You'll see," I said.

Elizabeth poked me in the ribs. "It's time," she whispered.

"Mom? Dad?" I said. "Can we go get some more popcorn?"

"Already?" Mom said. "Well, I guess so." She gave us both a dollar. "You two stay together, and hurry back."

"OK," we said.

We rushed down through the crowd and ran straight to the popcorn stand. Daria's mom was there, shoveling a bunch of kernels into the big popper. "Hi, Mrs. Brahms," I said.

"Hello, Jessamyn," Mrs. Brahms said. "Hello, Elizabeth."

"Is everything ready?" I asked.

"It sure is," said a voice behind me. It was Mr. Brahms. He was the man we saw giving the pony an apple.

"Come with me, Jessamyn," he said. "Everybody's waiting."

"Good luck," Elizabeth told me. "Break a leg."

I shivered. "I hope not," I said.

Mr. Brahms led me to the camper where the show riders get changed into their costumes. I was thinking about how sad Daria was in the circus.

"You know, Mr. Brahms," I said, "Daria's awfully lonely in the circus."

He looked surprised. "Really?" he said.

"Uh-huh. There aren't any other kids around," I pointed out. "You think maybe you could get her a sister or something?"

Daria's dad laughed. "I think I'd have to ask Mrs. Brahms about that," he said. "But if Daria's unhappy being in the circus, that's not good."

He opened the door to the camper. "Would you ask Daria to step outside for a moment?" he said to me.

Uh-oh. I hoped I hadn't got Daria in trouble. "Sure," I answered.

Inside the camper, all the show riders were ready to go. "Hi, everyone," I called. "Thanks for your help. I hope I don't mess up."

"Don't worry," said the Amazing Zara. She was the prettiest show rider. "You just remember how we practiced it yesterday, and you'll be fine."

Then Daria appeared out of nowhere. She was already in costume.

"Hey, Daria," I said. "Your dad wants to talk to you. He's right outside."

"OK," Daria said. "You better get ready quick! You don't want to be late for your big debut!"

A few minutes later, I was sitting outside the big top, just about to make my first circus appearance. I couldn't believe it!

"And now!" the ringmaster announced. "Please welcome Sweet Valley's own: the Amazing Jessamyn!"

Daria's dad pulled back the tent flap, and I rode Tony the pony right out into the spotlight. I felt beautiful and glamorous in my sparkling pink costume. The crowd cheered. I'd never been so thrilled in all my life!

I saw my family and friends in the bleachers. All their mouths were wide open in surprise.

Just like we'd practiced, all the other riders lined up at the back of the ring. They were standing on their ponies. I very carefully stood up on Tony's back. Then I held a big plastic hoop out in the air beside me.

When I was sure I had my balance, I cried out: "Ready!"

Daria rode right toward the hoop at top speed. At the very last second, she jumped. While the pony ran under the hoop, Daria flipped through it. She landed right on the pony's back again. It was perfect timing!

"Yay, Daria!" I cheered. The audience went wild.

One by one, the rest of the riders jumped through the hoop. I made sure I held it very steady. They were depending on me.

When they were all done, we lined up our ponics and took a bow. I waved to the audience, like I'd dreamed of doing. The applause was so loud, it sounded like the ocean. Elizabeth was right up front, cheering louder than anybody.

I couldn't have stopped smiling if I'd wanted to. I know that Great-

great-grandma Jessamyn would have been very proud of me.

The minute I got back inside the trailer, Daria grabbed me by the arm.

"Jessica!" she said. "My dad asked me if I want to quit the circus!"

"You're kidding!"

"And he said it's OK! He said he and Mom want me to be happy, no matter what! So they're going to get jobs on a ranch, and we'll have a real, regular home! Can you believe it?"

"That's great, Daria!" I gave her a big hug.

"I can't believe this is my last night in the circus," Daria said. She was grinning from ear to ear. "And your first, too! Maybe you can have my old job!"

"That's OK," I said. "I'm happy where I am."

"Yeah." Daria laughed. "So am I, now."

"You were great, Jess!" Elizabeth said. The circus was over, and we were all on our way out of the big tent.

"Yeah!" Lila and Amy agreed.

"You were wonderful, Jessica," Mom said. "You really looked like you belong in the spotlight."

"Well," I said, tossing my hair back, "I *do*. I'm a natural." Everybody laughed.

"You must be," Dad said. "Since you'd never even ridden a pony before tonight, I mean."

"Yeah," Steven said suspiciously. "How'd you pull that off?"

"I'll never tell," I said. I looked at Elizabeth. She laughed.

"Do *you* know, Elizabeth?" Mom asked.

Everyone waited for Elizabeth to